The Bard of Biscuit City

A Romantic New Age Mystery Rhyme

P. H. Newcombe

Published by Bard of BC Publishing, April 2019
ISBN: 9781999056605

Copyright © 2019 by P. H. Newcombe
All rights reserved. No part of this publication may be reproduced, stored in or introduced into a retrieval system, or transmitted, in any form, or by any means (electronic, mechanical, photocopying, recording or otherwise) without the prior written permission of the publisher. This book is sold subject to the condition that it shall not, by way of trade or otherwise, be lent, resold, hired out, or otherwise circulated without the publisher's prior consent in any form of binding or cover other than that in which it is published and without a similar condition including this condition being imposed on the subsequent purchaser.

Editor: P. H. Newcombe
Typeset: Greg Salisbury
Proofreader: Lee Robinson
Book Cover Design: P. H. Newcombe
Author Photo: P. H. Newcombe
Photo of P. H. Newcombe & Sharon Lee Watts: Brian Piitz

DISCLAIMER: This book is a work of fiction. Names, characters, places or incidents are either the product of the author's imagination or are used fictitiously. Any resemblance to actual persons, living or dead, events, or locales is entirely coincidental. Readers of this publication agree that neither P. H. Newcombe nor his publisher will be held responsible or liable for damages that may be alleged or resulting directly or indirectly from the reading of this publication.

Testimonials

"P. H. Newcombe has created a lovely and lively lyrical piece of storytelling, equal parts reverie, homily and simple old-fashioned fun. The Bard of Biscuit City is an allegorical lament; thoughtful and highly personal, a charming and engaging work of poetry for adults of all ages."
B. Miron, Master of Arts English Literature

"One cannot help but be struck by Mr. Newcombe's imaginative, creative writing in The Bard of Biscuit City. With rich descriptions of colorful scenes, complex characters and mysterious plot twists masterfully woven into a rhythmic tapestry, it evokes delight and wonder while raising the question, "Who, indeed, is the mysterious Bard of Biscuit City?"
Ralph Walker, Writer

"A return to story-telling! No need for a computer screen as this cast of characters leaps from the page vividly and hilariously. Your mind races to keep up with the subtle, yet, in your face twists and turns. I loved it. I want to have dinner with the voices in Mr. Newcombe's head."
Jim Shield, Actor, 5-Time World Champion Outrider, 4-Time Calgary Stampede Champion Outrider

"The Bard of Biscuit City reminded me of the precious gift and journey of Life: to live, love, laugh and cry through all of its ups, downs and in-betweens. Mr. Newcombe expresses it beautifully."
Sam Robert Muik, Actor, CBC web series "Hudson"

"God made him, and therefore let him pass for a man."

~Portia, the Merchant of Venice, ACT I, SCENE II

"Not marble nor the gilded monuments
of princes shall outlive this powerful rhyme."

~ SONNET 55

"Let those who are in favor of their stars
of public honor and proud titles boast
whilst I, whom fortune of such triumph bars…"

~SONNET 25

"Be still when you have nothing to say; when genuine passion moves you, say what you've got to say, and say it hot."

~ D. H. Lawrence

To the Reader

The Bard of Biscuit City is a menagerie of humor, romance, poetry, mystery, fantasy, allegory, a children's "Absey" story, New Age and Christian spirituality, with sundry allusions to contemporary literature, art and music.

It is an ode to William Shakespeare, a morality play with a salute to Monty Python's Flying Circus and tip of cap to the legend of King Arthur's Court and the Knights of the Round Table.

It's also my own story. The characters in this story represent aspects of many "personalities" rolled into one person, me, a unique human being in mind, body and soul expressing fragmented embodiments or elements of my divine masculine and feminine sides.

To this day, the debate continues about who William Shakespeare actually was. Was he a man or a woman? Could a man possibly write such fully developed female characters?

Was more than one person, male or female, involved in the writing? If so, how many? And whom? These questions have been asked - and fairly. I encourage curious readers to treat themselves to Robin Patricia Williams' wonderful book, *Sweet Swan of Avon*, for but a taste of what I mean.

Some readers find it hard to imagine how any human being could have written so prolifically and with such staggering brilliance and scope in such a short span of time. They ask: "Was Shakespeare even human?" It strikes me as possibly beyond human capability.

Harold Bloom, Bill Bryson and others have gifted us with diverse and brilliant analyses on Shakespeare's universalism and the many mysteries of the life and work of the one who wrote:

All the world's a stage,
And all the men and women merely players;
They have their exits and their entrances;
And one man in his time plays many parts,

His acts being seven ages. At first the infant,
Mewling and puking in the nurse's arms;
And then the whining school-boy, with his satchel
And shining morning face, creeping like snail
Unwillingly to school. And then the lover,
Sighing like furnace, with a woeful ballad
Made to his mistress' eyebrow. Then a soldier,
Full of strange oaths, and bearded like the pard,
Jealous in honor, sudden and quick in quarrel,
Seeking the bubble reputation
Even in the cannon's mouth. And then the justice,
In fair round belly with good capon lin'd,
With eyes severe and beard of formal cut,
Full of wise saws and modern instances;
And so he plays his part. The sixth age shifts
Into the lean and slipper'd pantaloons,
With spectacles on nose and pouch on side;
His youthful hose, well sav'd, a world too wide
For his shrunk shank; and his big manly voice,

> *Turning again toward childish treble, pipes*
> *And whistles in his sound. Last scene of all,*
> *That ends this strange eventful history,*
> *Is second childishness and mere oblivion;*
> *Sans teeth, sans eyes, sans taste, sans everything.*

> *As You Like It ~ Act II, Scene VII*

And there you have it.

The three fore-mentioned writers possess brilliant insights and pose fascinating questions and theories. I am no scholar, nor do I pretend to be. I'm just a star-struck fan of what sounds and feels to me like infinite wisdom shining through William Shakespeare's collected works. I say this because the moments are too many when my soul feels as if it has been touched by something true.

We all borrow from Shakespeare every day. William Shakespeare literally shaped most of modern human language, the "lion's share" of clichés we unconsciously parrot daily, as well as a large portion of human consciousness and culture.

Allusions to Shakespeare's works appear throughout my story. And please note: I use the word "sonnet" loosely, like an ode, poem or song. Some are veiled, some overt; some are red herrings, some breadcrumbs leading to the answer of that self-same mystery. Who really is the Bard? Of the 20 original human characters and two four-legged friends in The Bard of Biscuit City, one is the definitive Bard.

I hope the mystery is part of the tickle in the play.

The Bard of Biscuit City has a cast of characters plucked purely from my imagination. It is a fantasy world and should not be confused as anything but voices from within me. It is essentially a dream and a prayer; one of a fairer, kinder, world and planet where war, greed, hatred, fighting, disease, poverty, hunger and all expressions of fear are overcome by the power of love, a Love that comes from God, the Creator of All that Is.

A man can dream and believe in miracles. I do, and I will until the day I die.

Finally, writing this book has provided me with an important vehicle for self-expression in an evolving 12-year journey healing from prostate cancer and other life traumas that have impacted me; at least five brain concussions playing competitive hockey by age 23, subsequent episodic struggles with clinical depression and anxiety that still occur from time to time, spinal meningitis in my first year of life, and having loved and suddenly lost someone very dear to me more than 30 years ago now.

For reasons far beyond my understanding and more painful than I know how to put in words, I did not say the goodbye I wanted to. This book is dedicated to an impossibly beautiful woman I loved once upon a time in this life. She loved me dearly and told me so the last night we shared, though I did not know she was saying goodbye. I only understood in retrospect her foreknowledge she would soon be leaving.

When she left this world, part of me did too.

If, by writing and sharing this book, it helps anyone heal

from any form of trauma or pain, then this love letter, my goodbye, and before too long to be hello again, I will rest in peace knowing my love's labor was not lost, nor did I labor here in vain.

P. H. Newcombe

March 8, 2019

Cast of Characters

The King of Constant Worry
The Queen Fantatically Clean
The Prince of Sad Excuses
The Princess of Procrastination
The Earl of Good Advice
Jolie St. Germaine, Baker, Le Cafe Montreal
The Knights of Utter Nonsense:
1. Sir Rantsalot
2. Sir Bafflegab
3. Sir Groovy Two Shoes
4. Sir Lingo Clarifier
Am I the Dauphine? Evil Empress of New France
The Duke of Bad Decisions
The Duchess of Dirty Lies
The Man-Killer Mannequins
1. Anais Anon
2. Anouk
3. Antoinette
The Archbishop of Ucantelope
Small Talk Satan
Two Fools: BS & Mighty Boring
Applebert (Pony) & Wigglebob (Piglet)

Prologue

I remember the day Love met

It was summer, warm breeze in evening

And all the world serene

Was there in Commoner's Market… least likely of all

The King of Constant Worry

Met his Queen of Fanatically Clean

She spied his Worry

He spied her Beauty

They glanced

Then once again

Unseemly? Yes

Impossible? No

For this was Biscuit City

Was there King Worry's dream took wing

And in a heartbeat soared to Heaven

Then back in a moment that was self-same
Came his Sweet Clean Swan, his Song of Avon
Aroused by such a comely sight
Worry blushed and turned away
For Clean did dress so smart and bright
To this winsome one, he knew not what to say
But he thought again
And said, "I am King
Of all in Biscuit City
So why should I fret?
And fret yet more
I'll not leave adorned with pity!"
So Constant Worry swaggered forth
Steely Dan and bold with plot
But he worried still
Hair thinning so
Whilst his royal waist was thinning not
With curtsied bow of grace and style
Fair Lady of Anti-Eunuch

Did spy a speck of lint upon
Worry's Royal Purple Tunic!
"Tsk, tsk," she spake
"This shall not do for sake of royal duty!
For a King so fine and handsome
We will cleanse and press it firm, my Lord,
And spit-shine your royal booty!"
Well, Worry now had heard enough
Heart and loins picked clean as cherries!
So he cut to chase and shouted out
"By Fate, we shall be married!"
So this is how it all began
In the world of Clean and Worry
Time did stand still for all to see
Though perhaps the pair did hurry
May their dreams stay young
And rife with fun
And may Love's soul mates sit a pretty
As the moon rises bright

P. H. NEWCOMBE

O'er the sky above

The King and Queen of Biscuit City

ACT I: SCENE I

The city slept, then woke anew

And no one was amiss

Of how the world had tilted thus

With Love's first sweet Soul kiss

So the city went about its way

Baking biscuits every day

Large and small, soft and round

Some hard as clay baked in the ground

All were lovely, fresh and good

Made with butter, Love, and fired by wood!

Who am I, am I? You ask, I hear!

Who speaks of all of this?

I Am the Bard of Biscuit City!

Perchance a Mystery in a Mist

Here in time and life

In hopes and dreams

Sent here from far away

Well, not so much, if you tune me right

And let your Soul come out to play

Pray listen up, pray listen well

To the drum beat of these hearts

The King he had a single son

T'is here that we shall start

And the Queen she had a daughter

From a marriage in her past

Now two and two make four, I say

But could this family actually last?

The rumor was the lad was lacking

And little more than sad sack useless

So he was known in Biscuit City as

The Prince of Sad Excuses

And the girl soon would make a name

For her tardiness and golden mane

In no time she had made a splash

And found her special station

So throughout the land her name was nicked

Princess Procrastination

This worried Worry, who worried lots

About everything and more

While Clean did notice nothing

But the filth on every floor

Throughout the castle

In the streets

On countertops

Between the sheets

Where she kept her King of Constant Worry

Alive and kicking, motor purring

It was only there

The king was freed

From his furrowed brow

At Light speed

Then came one day

At dawn's first light

After being up most half the night

The King could not rise up this day

"So stay in bed," his wife did say

"I'm off you see, to scout out fakery!

And find the perfect biscuit bakery!"

"Sounds good, my love"

Said worn-out Worry

"Take your time,

No need to hurry

I'll be here when you get back

Unless I have a heart attack"

"Oh, you'll be fine!" winked sexy Clean

"You know I am your Biscuit Queen!

I'll get you up and standing tall

But first I'll grab our Princely Paul

And Princess Paula, rascal dear

Keep an eye on them

So have no fear!"

But the King was now fast asleep

Snoring like a bleating sheep

Clean kissed him on his forehead soft

And started on her way

To find the perfect biscuit for her love

On a perfect Biscuit City day

ACT I: SCENE II

The kindly Earl of Good Advice
Was waiting for his King
Wondering where he was that morn
And what the day might bring
He had bad news to gently break
About impending dangers
The King's relatives were coming
With wily ways no better strangers
The Duke of Bad Decisions
Was Worry's brother in New France
Where The Duchess of the Dirty Lie
Had snatched him by his underpants
She'd led him down a primrose path
Of lies, excess and sloth

But the Duke was helpless to her charms

As a bedazzled codling moth

They'd be broke as bums as sure as shite

And come a-begging for a handout

Of golden coins and croissants too

And God knows what else they might

Be up to next!

What dirty lie!

Or bad idea soon to follow!

Every time the pair came to town

T'were no visit from Apollo

Wild Compassion is quite grand

And Charity is fine

But these two were calamitous

So the King must draw the line

But the King was not there to hear

So the Earl could only wait and fear

As the barge moored out in Biscuit Bay

"Good Christ," he spake

"I'd better pray

Worry gets his fanny out of bed

Because Clean might drop them seeing red

If they meet her first in Biscuit City

T'will not be good

And war's not pretty!

For the Duchess of the Dirty Lie

Will spark a fire, and Clean's reply

Will be to clean their clocks right there

And smash relations past repair!"

"Good King!" he shouted

"Rise and Shine!

Coffee's on and biscuits fine!

Await they now with peach jam too!

Please my King, rise-aroo!"

But the King was out and dreaming fast

Of the kinds of fun that make love last

He could not hear while hard a-crashin'

Dreaming of Clean's fleshy passion

So while he dreamed I sent him this
Fair sonnet of a kind
That he'd remember when he woke
To raise his window blind:

You are the Beautiful Dance Key
Yes, you, and you know who You are
For the Light in your eyes lit Heaven beyond
And ignites this world and its stars
In this river of time, shallow and deep
Hearts run cold and are blank
Staring off in a world
Torn from Love that is near
With thoughts that have fear but to thank
In mysterious twists and turns on the way
They drown in one spot
Neither moved nor can sway
Until one and by One
They reach the near shore

Where You wait for them smiling
And unlock the door
To a Ballroom so grand
He cannot believe
How long He's been gone
How short Her reprieve
From a truth that is done
And always was free
The truth of His One, the only, the She
The Truth of The Beautiful Dance Key

ACT I: SCENE III

The Duke of Bad Decisions

And The Duchess of Dirty Lies

Were less in-laws than outlaws

And in truth but royal spies

Employed by Am I the Dauphine?

The evil Empress of New France

Their aim was to rip-off croissants

And thwart this newly wed romance

The Dauphine long feared King Worry

She knew his heart not well

Because the shadow side of Light is dark

Her inner space was living hell

When her flagship Maid of Driftwood

Arrived in Biscuit Bay

The Knights of Utter Nonsense

The Good Earl sent upon their way
Sir Bafflegab, Sir Rantsalot
And Sir Groovy Two Shoes too
Led the charge to Biscuit Bay
To bring the French a bon adieu!
They rode like heroes on their way
To save a Hamlet caught on fire
While closing on their hastened heels
Charged Sir Lingo Clarifier
And though Lingo's steed Spiff Lacking
Ran like a lollygagging boulder
Sir Lingo had the quickest wheels
Upstairs upon his shoulders
For he had a way with words you see
By Fate he had a special talent
For making utter sense of none
With his brothers who were gallant
But less than swift as diplomats

Or relating to the fairer sex
The tin pots that they wore as hats
Were indeed much more complex
Than their best laid plans
For "What's for lunch?"
Or even what thought might come next!
"The French will fry!" cried Rantsalot
"We'll cook those bums in oil!"
"Or a Bum Boo Bisque!" yelled Bafflegab
"Boiled on Biscuit City soil!"
"Hell, that's got no taste," said Two Shoes
"It's not beaucoup one sweet bit!
How about rotisserie?
Slow cooked froggy on a spit!"
Three Knights of Utter Nonsense
Did howl with joie de vivre
While Sir Lingo went right batty
Scratching head just to conceive
Of a plot to keep his brethren

From screwing up the Earl's directions
And get the French folk back at castle
Without Clean's intervention
Diplomacy for family ties
These were the orders on this day
Get the Duke and Duchess to the King
Then see what next would play
While on the Maid of Driftwood
The French pair was coyly waiting
With weapons of their very own
Three of a higher octane rating
The Mannequin Man-Killers
Were made up beyond breathtaking
Their attire was more than casual
About that there was no faking
Shapes of hips and bottoms
Could make three wise men faint
Waists were tiny wisps of air
Breastplates to turn a patron saint

Anais, Anouk and Antoinette
The Man-Killers One Two Three
This was AI tech before its time
Made by Am I the Dauphine?
"It's soon time to go ashore,"
Said the Duchess to the Duke
"Wind up our Damsel Mannequins
Set to Maximum Rebuke!"
"Are you sure, my love?" asked the arbiter
Of countless less than wise decisions
That might be a bit of overkill
A stratagem of imprecision"
"It's up to you," the Duchess said
"I'll leave it to your call
But if we fail our heads will roll
Instead of Worry's tete to fall!"

ACT I: SCENE IV

Queen Clean, Sad Prince and Paula
The Princess of Procrastination
Were doing cartwheels in the street
Having found sweet jubilation!
They'd searched good Biscuit City
For the finest fare of all
And at last success
Was savored best
At Le Café Montreal
From doggy treats to fresh eclair
It was all anyone could want
But the piece de resistance was
The famed "Butter Bomb Croissant"
So Clean cleaned out their stock tout suite

And hired the baker on the spot

To do all the royal baking

From that moment forth and not

One moment sooner could it have been

For down at Biscuit Bay

The French had landed on the beach

Mannequins all set to play

With the Knights of Utter Nonsense

But not on "Maximum Rebuke"

They'd been switched to clever "Femme Fatale"

With cleavage fit for Marmaduke

The Knights of Utter Nonsense

Would be putty in their mittens

For Sir Lingo's three Swords of Steel

Had never seen such sexy kittens

When the landing ramp was lowered

And the runway models strut ashore

The Knights' tongues were switched to silent

No they wagged not one bit more

Bafflegab was baffled

Two Shoes was a fog

And Rantsalot was panting

Memory begging to be jogged

For the right words he should say now

About frying up the French

And all that he could muster was

"Damn… I wish…

I had a Paris catwalk wench!

To make my blood rise every night!

To take me to the moon!

I wonder if I could interest one

In a lovely macaroon?

Down at that Café Montreal

I know they've got some dandies there

And I know they've got those 'crawsongs'

And dainty chocolate eclair!"

Yes, Rantsalot spilled his guts

As he was often wont to do

And when the Mannequins said

"Oui Monsieur!

When shall we rendezvous?"

Bafflegab went batty

Two Shoes checked his feet

Rantsalot's face turned bright

As a crimson baby beet!

Sir Lingo'd not seen this before

Thus it caused him consternation

For suddenly he ciphered

A new threat to their station

As protectors of the King of Worry

And the Queen of Crazy Clean

This was a wrinkle unexpected

Dynamics unforeseen

The planets now were dancing

Love was in the air

God help us all, thought Lingo

With this Cosmic Love Affair!

ACT I: SCENE V

The King of Constant Worry

Was now an up and at 'em atom!

News of the French arrival

He'd had time to fully fathom

His heart was soft light to the core

Kindness his ne'er-daunted chore

"Surely, Earl, my trusted friend

We can find a way to extend

Ourselves to give relations dear

Food and gold, if they fear

Not enough to keep them fed

And out of Am I's bankrupt bed"

"But my goodly king," said the Earl

"Though your intentions are but pure

Our coffers and our pantries
Are not well stocked, I'm sure
The winter's nigh upon us now
And what if next year brings
A harvest less than bountiful
You know, Fate's a funny thing
You can never have a nest egg
That is too large or too fine
To fall back on when days grow hard
Amidst uncertain times"
King Worry stroked his furry chin
And nodded in agreement
"Well, we'll take it slow with the clan
And make sure there's no mistreatment"
Then suddenly the door flew open
And in rushed the Biscuit Queen
"My darling I have found it!
My honey bun! My dream!
Oh, take a bite dear love of mine

Tear a piece off of my biscuit!

It's not some ritzy cracker, hon

Or some dried up boring friskuit!

It's the Butter Bomb Croissant

From Le Café Montreal!

And when it comes to biscuits in the city

It's the final port of call!"

Clean jammed the bun in Worry's mouth

And he mowed down on the treat

Then he gave the Queen a playful slap

On her apple bottom sweet

The Earl got up and took his leave

Because things were getting rather steamy

The King and Queen had started necking

Eyes were misting sexy dreamy

So he tiptoed out of the room

And shut the door on his way out

Just in time

Because right behind

Came Sir Lingo with a shout

"Good Advice! Oh Earl of mine!

We've got ourselves a situation!

The Knights of Utter Nonsense

Are on a permanent vacation!

They've resigned good Earl

They've gone AWOL

They're on a dangerous excursion!

They have lost their minds

Slight as they were

And signed up

For French immersion!"

ACT I: SCENE VI

Serendipitous random run-ins
Seemed the order of the day
Rare success or divine planning
Is it possible to say?
Which is which?
Or what is what?
When two worlds and stars collide
Ah, but there are prizes worth attaining
Where hearts and souls and wills abide
What remains is always who and why
In this grand mystery of life
Five Ws and how it works
Is what's to music drum and fife
Prince Paul and Princess Paula

Were yet another case in point

How Fate had set their paths on course

Like a perfect dovetail joint

They'd bailed on Paula's mother dear

After Le Café Montreal

"Let's take a stroll down by the bay"

Said Prince of Excuses Paul

"I'm kind of tired, maybe later"

Said Paula with a sigh

"Mother said don't be late for dinner

It's like I'm still in junior high!

Oh, it's such a royal pain

With her lectures almost daily

I'm tired of all this nagging

God, she treats me like a baby!"

"You're telling me," said the Prince

"Father rides me all the time

Says I've an alibi for everything

And I can change them on a dime!"

"We both could use a break you know,"
Said the girl through teeth a-grating
"Can you imagine how they'd freak out
If they knew that we are dating!
Oh, if we only had a looking glass
To see what we should do!"
"Now there's a plan'" said Paulie
"A psychic seer or guru!
To help us figure out what's best
And how to steer our way
Through this mess!
All this worry, all this clean
It's no way for us to live!
Let's pray we get the help we need
Something here has got to give!"
So while plotting they kept walking
And ended up at Biscuit Bay
Where the Dirty Duchess waited
And greeted them with

"Que est-ce que c'est?
You two look so worried!
Oh Mon Dieu, my dear Mon Dieu!
Pray tell what is on your mind?
Your dearest auntie loves you
And I'm here to help divine
What everyone needs the most
Here in Biscuit City
Paul, you're growing up so handsome
And Paula's truly drop-dead pretty!
These faces long just will not do
Come let's go! Let's hurry!
It's been too long since the Duke and I
Have seen the King of Constant Worry!
And we hear his bride the Queen of Clean
Is the fairest of the fair
And we hear she has a penchant
For a spic and span affair!"
"Oh that's for sure," said Paula

"You could eat off the palace floor
Except the King would worry that you'd die
Of a germ or two for sure"
The Duchess howled with laughter
And slapped her knee with glee
"Oh Dear Dieu, my pretty ones
Things need to lighten up I see!
It's time to party hearty
To let the hair down as you say
When the Duke gets here
With the wine we brought
We shall raise a glass and play!"

ACT I: SCENE VII

Anais, Anouk and Antoinette

Decked out Celebrity A-List

Had three Knights of Utter Nonsense

Deftly dangling on their wrists

Bafflegab bound to Anais

Groovy Two Shoes to Anouk

Rantsalot to Antoinette

All being watched by the Grand Duke

He'd ciphered keep an eye on all

Freshly minted prototypes

The first models of the Dauphine

Programmed to early archetypes

Femme Fatale worked perfect

A seductress of pure lethal beauty

Combining brains and looks and cunning hooks

And just a dash of snooty

Le Café Montreal was closed

After the Queen cleaned out their stock

The baker, Jolie St. Germaine

Now royal baking 'round the clock'

She set pleasures of the table

To overflowing horn of plenty

For what would be a family feast

Working like a spinning jenny

In attendance was BCs high priest

A kind of local royal pope

Sporting a name that aptly fit

Archbishop of Ucantelope

He held himself above all subjects

Having dibs on straight to God

With great wealth in shiny nuggets

He saw himself one Holy Rod

When all were finally greeted

Introduced and seated round

The King proposed a toast to all

That health and happiness abound

"Hear, Hear!" all cried

"Here's to Biscuit City's King!

Long Live the Royal Monarch!

To him our praise we sing!"

But out of thin air

The King did snare

A sound like a question mark

The priest harumphed

And cleared his throat

Or perhaps it was a fart

"King Worry, you forgot to pray

For God's blessing on my meat

And this wine that I've before me

Smells like a Frenchman's feet!"

"Hey Ucantelope!" said Queen Clean

"How about you take a hike?

Better yet, hit the road!

And if 'Get it?' you don't quite,

I could tap a message for your Holy Mess

Using knuckles as Morse Code!"

The Mannequins did LOL

And the Knights they followed suit

While the Bishop arched his unibrow

And scowled all old world coot

King Worry was aghast, and how

Unsure of what to say

Until the Earl of Good Advice chimed in

"Perhaps we ought to pray

It cannot hurt in times like these

As faith must have its place

To bridge the path between us all

And smooth the way to Grace"

"Thank you Earl," said Loco-Pope

"Your advice is wise and good

I bless this eve and this food

Even mouths that need some soap!"
The Queen of Clean shot looks to kill
Worry calmed her with his footsie skill
And so the feast at last got underway
"Let's get down!" cried the Mannequins
"Qui vivra verra!"
Oo-la-la… let's partay!!"

ACT I: SCENE VIII

From Angel food to wild mandrake

Passion does all Love's rules break

And Oui Oui Monsieur

The French wine was the bomb!

"Let not the weekend go by

We must dance and paint the town!"

Said Rantsalot, all hot to trot

While hustling like a Clown

"Oo la la, bebe," purred Antoinette

"For to paint it in the raw?

Mes ami et moi

Bien nous desirons

A bon menage a trois!"

Rantsalot was clueless now

Gabber's brain took a wee flier

Two Shoes was also out to lunch

But not Sir Lingo Clarifier

He could read between the lines

And did not need a French translator

To see where things were heading

Which was south of the equator!

Meanwhile in the corner

The Prince and Princess snuck a smooch

But it did not flee Worry's eye

Even after quaffing too much hooch

Thank God, he thought, my lovely Queen

Is busy with the French

How will I break the news to Clean?

Without causing teeth to clench

Or fur to fly as metaphor

Or Dido much to pay

She'll garnishee their stipends

And they'll not get out to play

No, she'll ground them fast

In their rooms

Tethered to their desks

Where she'll make them write

A thousand times

I'm under house arrest!

Just say no to holding hands!

Just say no to kissing!

Make a baby and it's hell to pay

Paulie's head will go a-missing!

Now the Duchess of Foul Falsehoods

From the corner of her eye

Was devising how to play her pawns

How to squeeze and splay and spy

A house divided always falls

She knew this to be true

And there were many means to her end

All less than derring-do

The Duke of Bad Decisions

Her husband and soul mate

Had been right about the Mannequins

Femme Fatale for Section Eight

The Knights were rooked

Their biscuits cooked

Buns buttered on both sides

And with the teen romance heating up

She could feel cool victory vibes

But the Queen of the Obsessive Clean

Was no weak willed adversary

She was quick of wit

Perchance whacked a bit

With a temper righteous scary

"So what's the game here, Duchess?

I smell you're up to tricks!

You and the Duke are naught but trouble

And straight headed for deep six

If you mess with us"

Warned she who'd fuss

How best to mop the floor

With family heels above their heads

Sans esprit de corps!

"Oh Mon Dieu, Mon Dieu!

Dear Queen of Clean!

The past is past

All's well at last

We come wishing only this

That you and Constant Worry

Taste alone but Fate's sweet kiss"

"We'll see," said Clean

"Time will tell

What the future holds for all

But mark my words

Make one false move

Et tu mange le cannonball!"

The Duke stepped in and said, "Whoa now,

Seems we're none too welcome here

Best off we go into the night

Back to Biscuit City pier!"

A wake-up call then arrived

For the Knights of the Slow Twitch

The models sudden "Bonsoir, boys"

Came like they'd flipped a frosty switch

Soon the French were gone again

The evening overdone

Worry called the Earl close to him

Whispered, "We meet tomorrow morn

I know I can do more here

There is need here I can sense

We must find what is needed most

And spare Love no expense"

ACT I: SCENE IX

The King slept not a nod or wink
Rose that morning weary tired
While the Queen was scrubbing out the sink
And growing clean inspired
Snail mail sat on Worry's desk
Sheeted like thin ice
Where was his trusty counsel?
His sterling Earl of Good Advice
This cannot wait, said the King
I've business much to do
Let me open up a package here
Hands-on is tried and true
He took a box of royal hue
Held it up to view it pretty

It had lettered on its violet lid
"The Bard of Biscuit City"
Worry worried first
Who could this be?
A bard he'd not heard word of?
What might this bode for Destiny?
What might this mean for courtly love?
The note attached was in plain sight
The script clear in golden ink
The Earl arrived, took note of all
Then Worry did aloud bethink
"Come sit Earl, come listen close
Let me read a sonnet to you, sir
It's from The Bard of Biscuit City
Some unknown raconteur"
"Please do, my King," said Good Advice
"I've no doubt the timing's right
Pray lift your voice and share with me
We will see what comes to light"

As I leave you, Love

Slow-leave taking

Born anew

I move on Understood

Where the deepest well awaits

Horizon grows

Ending dreams of days

This clay heart

It stays behind, behind

Behold I pass through Heaven's gates

Beauty and light

Past forgotten fights

Present face-to face

This final day my better way

Has found its full embrace

On angels wings

I rise to meet

The One who knew me first

She holds me to her Breast again

He has quenched my mortal thirst

This lovely thing

Emptied now

Of all it once became

Of its strength and hope

Broken dreams and love

My body leaves and I remain

As I Leave you, Love

Slow-leave taking

Born anew

I move on Understood

Where the deepest well awaits

Horizon grows

Ending dreams of days

This clay heart

It stays behind, behind

Behold I pass through Heaven's gates

This lovely thing
Emptied now
Of all it once became
Of its strength and hope
Broken dreams and love
My body leaves and I remain

Worry's eyes began to tear
The King was shaken to the core
"T'is Death he speaks of kindly Earl
Is Time knocking at my door?"
"It's a warning, Sire
Yes, I'm sure
There are those that mean you harm
But have no fear you'll win the day
It's not time to sell the farm
Your work's not done

There's much here left to do

And you've no time for faint self-pity

We must find this Bard and find him fast

For the Fate of Biscuit City!"

ACT II: SCENE I

Hark, who goes there?

The Knights of Utter Nonsense!

Now marching triple overtime

While straddling a humble fence

Not of their means or making

Taking liberties or favors

They were resting in a purgatoire

Of life's most unkind flavor

"It's hard to get they play, they play!"

Said Bafflegab aloud

"No, it's worse than that

It's Bye Bye John!"

Said Rantsalot less proud

Two Shoes spied a scuff upon

His finest leather pair

"Shite," he scowled, "First the wench,

Now my shoes, next I'll lose my hair!"

Sir Lingo watched his lads' poor plight

And he felt for them a bit

But he knew that the day was young

Without clue to know of it

Or that the Earl and King were coming

Double riding Pearly's steed

To send his Knights on sacred quest

Of greatest royal deed

Cool café scenes

Hot clubs at night

Every two-bit dive and salon pretty

Could be the haunt of he they want

The cryptic Bard of Biscuit City

It took Sir Lingo half the morn

To explain the task they brought

For the Knights of Utter Nonsense

Had let their minds get caught

On clubs, and bars and coffee shops

Where pretty wenches love to hang

And where the super model Mannequins

Were sure to boomerang

Back in their lives

Hip-hip hooray!

Time to get this party started

So the shaking and the twisty baking

Started up just past noon lunch

And the Knights of Utter Nonsense

Were off and running on a hunch

ACT II: SCENE II

The King told all to his Queen

And hark, his Worry spread

Queen Clean proclaimed with gusto

"Damn French,

I'll see them dead!"

"We cannot strike," said Worry

"We cannot start a war

Not over biscuits, gold or croissants

We must find this troubadour"

"Are you sure of this?" asked the Queen

"His tone was mettle weak

And impending death

Well, that's a stretch

He's a wee bit dramatique!"

"No, my love, I feel it

I know this much is true

My life is now in jeopardy

The Bard's been sent to see me through

In this time of strife and peril

What is best you feel?

Hold a gala in his honour?

Entertain Achilles heel?

He would have to come

He'd have no choice

Chance another claim his work

And that is fraught with folly

For attention trollops lurk

You know Clean Dream my guess is

By golly this might work!"

Clean thought and said,

"Sure as ghosts are dead

Writers one and all are vain

I'll get Jolie to bake up a grand

Of 'Butter Bombs Insane!'
That along with title
No real Bard could resist
He'll show his face and come clean
Without need of arm to twist!"
The King he smiled
"My wife, you're wild!
You're as brilliant as you're a beauty!"
"Ah, my dear," said his Scrubber near
"You're my King! And you're a cutie!"
"We will make it so
My darling Clean!
Mark my word this moment clear!
The Bard of Biscuit City
Will have no choice but to appear!"

ACT II: SCENE III

Let Me Explain and Princess Stalling

Were plotting on their own

The earth's gravity was falling

To doubled teenage pheromones

Awakened to a sense of What You Will

They figured, "Let's elope!"

No need to consult Mom and Pops

"This idea's just the dope!"

So they climbed out of their window

Commandeered a royal carriage

They took the reins of runaways

And made a vow of royal marriage

Just as soon as we cipher

Where we're ought to run

We're not exactly faceless

And getting caught will not be fun

We'll be on KP cleaning crew

And our penmanship will flourish

House arrest 'til Freedom 35

May not this romance nourish

So heads or tails

North or south

Was east or west best to wander?

Without a compass, map or plan

These were questions left to ponder

But time was short, patience shorter still

So the pair set on their way

They got lost at the first corner

Carriage bound for Biscuit Bay

When in doubt do twist and shout

Take the sledge and crack the seed!

Find the kernel, pop the cork

Celebrate Love's holy deed!

The in-laws said, "Bon idee!
Elopement? C'est romance!"
The pair could come and shack up
In a cool castle in New France
"But first you have a job to do,"
Said the Duchess of Untruth
"We need to test your loyalty
We need some living proof
You must go back for now my loves
We need eyes and we must hear
Of King Worry's every move
His every fart and every fear"
Sappy Duke had switched remote
So the king was safe for now
Bad D was driving Lies insane
They started quarrelling full row!
Meanwhile teenage heads went spinning
So much to comprehend
How swanky would the boutiques be

In Paris's high end?

How good was the café noir?

Foie gras et tourtiere?

And how grand were the silken threads

That they would surely wear?

Paul and Paula danced and sang

The Duke now slept alone

While the Mannequins applied some

Cosmetics of their own

Filing nails to daggers

Flogging lashes fresh

Tip Top was the shape of things

Well-sculpted marble flesh

All smooth upon the surface

All glistening and taut

For the Knights of Utter Nonsense

Who they'd spied down at the dock

Looking under dirty berths

Barrels and a boat

Said Anouk to the Duchess

"Duke's asleep… see if it doth float?"

The Duchess smiled, "Ooo-la la

You are a true Mad Hatter!

Take the kids ashore tout suite!

And set sail pitter-patter

If it does not drift healthy

If it does not gist good

If it feels like now or never

Or not even how it should

Sink the barge and swim ashore

The ocean will see fit

Men of Steel sink swiftly

I say let's be done with it!"

ACT II: SCENE IV

Behold the Art of Manliness

Raise a statue to your Thor

Tip a hat to your Adonis

Slow clap your hands to Lesley Gore

Style, savoir-faire and steel

Stir rollicking behavior

The Knights caught sight of Mannequins

And sang praises to their Savior

When the Mannequins came strutting tall

Three Knights didst sing a free for all!

I've got chain-mail undies

Stuck to my knightly butt

And I've got table manners

That would make you all throw up
I've got nothing substantial
In between my ears
Hell, I've got less class
Than a donkey's ass
In a herd of one-eyed steers!
Oh, if I get obnoxious
You can put me in my place!
And if I get unruly
You can mace me in the face!
But if I get a woman
You can kiss your ass goodbye!
'Cause makin' love to women
Sure beats drinkin' with the guys!

I've got Kalvin Culvert blue tights
Pre-shrunk and pre-stunk
And though my IQs none too high
I'm still a Biscuit City Hunk

With something substantial
Here on my near Farside
Hell, I've got me an ass
That's right world class
And I sure know how to ride!

So, if I get obnoxious
You can put me in my place!
And if I get unruly
You can mace me in the face!
But if I get a woman
You can kiss your ass goodbye!
'Cause makin' love to women
Sure beats drinkin' with the guys!

The Mannequins weren't laughing
But Nonsense did not care
All it could see was Paradise
Perchance a bungalow to share

No more nights of utter solo
Silent jumping one's own bones
Staring at a plastered ceiling
Swallowing the sad blue feeling
It's been one more night alone

No, no matter how far away
Or where a Sacred Fool may roam
He always hopes to come back
Where precious once was known
To forest green country fields
And forever blue city skies
To the bed where once she loved me
From sunset until sunrise
No matter how far away
Or where a Sacred Fool may roam
Come back, come near
My love, my dear
To the place that we called home

ACT II: SCENE V

Timely genuflection

May get you far in life

Ah, for total bliss and harmony

Best agree man with your wife

There is no point in shouting

Much less bursting at the seams

No vantage found in pouting

No infant tantrums marred by screams

It's best to know the lay

Of any landscape, lake or moor

Know when to keep your trap well shut

And bolt the castle door

"The night is near," said the King

"Clean your details are all set

For the Bard of Biscuit City

And the award he must accept

From me, the King

To he, the Bard

An honour and a vow

To all in Biscuit City

Friend and foe

Here and Now!

I, the King of Constant Worry

Give my word this day

Not to blather on too long

But I've got some things to say"

Clean rolled her eyes like azure dice

"Worry get down to the meat!

Don't go on about yourself dear,

Dive in spritely with both feet!"

"But Clean, my love, are you sure

The Bard will take our tasty bait?

Butter bomb croissants and peach jam

May not roust or instigate

Some gypsy bachelor poet

That is sending me these sonnets

First in my dreams

And now by day

As if my life depends upon it!

We may need more to offer

We may need more to coax

This Bard of Biscuit City

What if he's shy in front of folks?

What if he has sudden stage fright?

Perchance he has a cold?

He might be late in traffic!

Or smoking Acapulco Gold!

What if his wife's in labor?"

Worry paused and took a breath

He spied Clean shining china

Her face as pale as Death

And then the King mused aloud

"Perchance he's not a man, dear

What if the Bard has a vagina?

Maybe he's a she, you know

With horny hots for your Worry

I'm kind of cute from all I hear

Oh, the lines are all so blurry!"

Well, that was it

Clean did flip!

Fine china flew like arrows!

"I'll kill the bitch

If that's the case

A crush I could abide

But hot to trot for Worry?

I'll have the Witch's hide!!

What might the good Earl say?

Or Ucantelope's no Pope?

The Four Knights of Less than Clever?

I don't fight no rope-a-dope!"

"All I know is this, my dear"

Said Worry trying to calm his ruffled love

"The butter bomb croissant with jam

Best be the right kid glove"

ACT II: SCENE VI

Sirs Rantsalot, Bafflegab

And the cool one, Groovy Two Shoes

Were gurgling now a bubbly tune

Called the Slowly Drowning Blues

AI Mannequins hate getting wet

It messes with their wiring

And why bother if one can slay

Without a girl perspiring!

Costly is the kind of sight

Blind to what may be

When walking down a gang plank

With AI Mannequins times three

While on their way down to the bottom

The Knights did not despair

They'd passed ditch and don training

And soon were coming up for air

Free of heavy armor

They broke wave to light above

And saw the Mannequins ashore

Heading straight to push and shove

There was no time to think

Sink or swim it had to be

Dog paddle, crawl or butterfly

Take your pick of the three

And picture then near naked Knights

With but codpiece to their names

Soon bare bummed ass-less chaps they were

At Worry's Globe on Thames

Where Clean had set the contest

To cinch the title pretty

And claim the rightful owner

As The Bard of Biscuit City

When a man has lost his armor

His sword and ride and shield

There's not much steel left to swing

And even less to wield

When it's open mike in near nude

And a sample of your prose

A poem or a sonnet

Some kind of purple overdose

Is what the Queen is asking

From any in the crowd

And all you know is nonsense

Things can get a little loud

And don't forget the baking

Lest we forget the grand first prize

A thousand Butter Bomb Croissants

With peach jam, no surprise!

The show was set to go at eight

But would it even fly?

The Duke and Duchess in the offing

Man-Killers on Bonzai!

Meanwhile Jolie St. Germaine
Was baking croissants not ad hoc
More Butter Bombs incoming
With each tick and with each tock
The King and Queen sat waiting
Oddly quiet as could be
While the Earl of Good Advice
Was mum on all that he did see
The Archbishop of Ucantelope
Saw the Prince and Princess necking
And he decided that was quite enough
"Oh dear, are they dirty pecking?"
So there it was, the ploy was fab
Curtain set to rise then fall
One by one they'd get a stab
At being Liege of Poets all
The "Sonnet Off" was starting
The Bard's sloping trough departing
Magic was free falling

Will's Sonnet 12 a-calling

Portia had shape-shifted

Now her turn to be a-gifted

With quill and quire

Dove Inspired

Five Roses being sifted

Fairy to your Puck

Prithee hither Lady Luck!

To you I am indentured

And I know that 12 is getting old

But watch my cards of sleight unfold

And dance with us far-adventured!

ACT II: SCENE VII

Rantsalot was up first

Nervous as a groom

He was feeling pretty naked

Searching for a nom de plume

Small Talk Satan, I am he!

I'll kill you quick as quack

Just don't wind me up on good caffeine

Or smoke me up on crack!

No, I ain't Claude Akins

And I'm no Fred Estaire

I'm just a knight in shining armor

Who's losing all his hair!

I don't know any big words

I'm not a whining wuss!
And you may not differentiate
My bum bum from my puss!
I need an epic muffin
Build me a nuclear slow cooker
And no, I'm not making hay
With the city's happy hooker!

Queen Clean had heard about enough
"Rantsy, that's just fine
Small Talk Satan maybe
But you're not the Bard this time
Say are you missing something?
You look a little thin
And if I'm not mistaken
Have you been making time to swim?"
"Yes, Queen Clean, my codpiece
Got parted from my suit
I thought I'd bought the Big One

But she didn't give a hoot!"

"She?" said the Earl aloud

"To whom do you refer?

Are we talking skinny-dipping?

While on duty there, good sir?"

"Well, my Early Pearly Earl

I cannot tell a lie!

I think my date she pushed me in

Didn't even say goodbye!"

"Who's up next?" said the King

"Let's move along, now, now"

He was getting worried time was short

And he'd miss the Bard somehow

"How about Sir Two Shoes?

Our groovy stylish rake

He's groovy lean, always clean

And never on the take!"

"Let's hear something from the French"

Whispered Clean to her Worry

"I think Rantsy likes the tall wench

She's one twisted-looking furry!"

"Are you sure my love?" said the King

"Yes, I suppose you might be right

The Bard could be a dummy

We'll hear from the French tonight!"

ACT II: SCENE VIII

A thousand butter bomb croissants
The Duke of Bad Decisions thought
Should please Am I the Dauphine?
Certain war had been averted
Liar's ploy had been subverted
In the nick of time on Worry's dime
To kill a fateful fray
Seated in the cheap seats
He figured rip some tasty Keats
Then I'll easy be the Bard of Ballyhoo!
It really shouldn't take too much
'Cause Biscuit City poets suck
Their sonnets smell a lot like rudy poo
But next he shouted, "Antoinette!"

And switched her to "Anglais Coquette"
Seeing golden croissants gifted him this way
"Let's hear it girl," said wary Clean
"Get up here furry, sight unseen!
We've got all night if that is what it takes"
"I've got a sonnet!" cried Crash Test Dummy
"It's short and sweet and for my honey
For Rantsalot, my sweetie sugar cakes!"

Rantsy come on down
To ye olde dance hall
Let's cinque-a-pace
Real proud and tall
Bring your baby blues
And your big strong arms
Bring your dancing shoes
And your special charms
You can forget tomorrow
'Cause we'll do it right

Let's sleep all day
And dance all night!

Let's feel our way
Through the do-si-dos
Feel it from our heads
To our baby toes
Feel our way
Through the ins and outs
Feel our way
Through the twists and shouts
Yeah, we'll feel our way
Through the left foot right
Let's sleep all day
And dance all night!

Well, the Ranting Boy could not hide
His mighty admiration
"She's the Bard!" he spake

Slow clapping drake

While airing all before the nation!

The crowd went wild!

Rants went red

Exit stage in lesser head

So he took off like a silly boff undressed!

"My turn next!" said Anouk

"May I approach the royal bench?

Sir Groovy Two Shoes with me

I want to be his wedded wench!"

God of Thunder

Spawn of Thor

Take your pick

Either or

The house came down

And everyone said, "YES!!"

Ale did flow

Fine biscuits flew

Cool hats were in the air

Sir Groovy Two Shoes

Was a-dancing

Official Downtown Buckaroo!

ACT II: SCENE IX

But Bafflegab then went berserk

Charged up and took the floor

His codpiece still a-dripping

Leaving a trail that caused a roar

There's nothing like buck naked Knights

With a penchant for the natter

Baff got right to it

No bush to beat

And broke into naughty chatter!

Something in here stinks

And I don't know what it is

That underwear you're burning

Is it mine or is it his?

I know it's not my color
It's surely not my size
And now I see it up in flames
And teardrops in your eyes
I told you so, my darling
When I sashayed through the door
That God had made me different
That I know for sure
And I know I ain't no Steely Dan
But I've got news for you
That underwear you're burning there
Is big enough for two

"The Bard! The Bard!" screamed the crowd
But the King held up his hand
"Go easy on the sauce, now folks
Sir Groovy take the stand!"
With Two Shoes changed to Dapper Dan
He stepped forward, cleared his throat

And looking all a rich king's ransom
Anouk owned her sleek frock coat!
She stood beside her Groovy Sir
Curtsied to the King and Queen
"Let's hear this groovy stylish pair"
Said Worry to his Clean
"Two Shoes give us what you've got
Hold nothing back in fear
Either proffer sonnet piping hot
Or perchance to coax a tear"
"I will my King," said Two Shoes
"I wrote it from my heart
It's not the greatest masterpiece
Or classic work of art
It's just a dream I had once
When I was staring in a mirror
I was shining my shoes upside down
When suddenly appeared
A vision of another time

Another place, another land
The snow had softly fallen
I know it's hard to understand
It makes no sense, but well, what's new?
Heartache has been my life
It's not easy here in human skin
I really love Anouk, my wife!"
Set to pour his heart out
Sir Groovy's hands, well they did shake
Though he could slay a dragon in his sleep
Anouk set his knees to quake
He gazed on like Nellie Nervous
Then she whispered,
"Take your time, babe, don't you hurry"
Two Shoes now knew how it felt
To be the King of Constant Worry!
So when Two Shoes started rhyming
His feet felt free and feathered light
He took Anouk by wedded hand

And they waltzed into the night

Great old tree

Bent-limbed and frozen

She stands alone

Near wooden fences

Stitched over country fields

Over fields that once lay sewn

With threads of hay

Pushed through patches of snow

The brown earth quilted white

The sky so gray

The wind so cold

Another day turns into night

The air it sings

The air it swirls

Just once the Moon breaks through

The clouds that part

Then close again

It's true the wind can be so cruel

Anouk and I

We watch these things

Through window's frosted pane

It's warm inside

The cedar kindling snaps

And the fire it entertains

And the wine we drink

Is bright and clear

Like lovers' eyes in candlelight

And in the morning

We will still be here

As another day turns into night

The groundlings stunned to sniffles

Scant snorts or sputters heard

The King he wiped a tear away

The Queen stared out rather stirred

The Earl of Good Advice

Was lost for words for once

Ucantelope the cleric said

"Christ, I thought he was a dunce"

"Where'd Groovy learn to write like that?"

Said Sir Lingo Clarifier

"With such clarity and cadence

He'd have made a fine town crier"

The Duke and Duchess too were moved

Not exactly ordinaire

It made them pause and wonder

About the state of these affairs

"This seems too good to be

It seems your call was right"

She smiled and squeezed her husband's hand

"What's up your sleeve tonight?"

"I've no clue," said the Duke

"Masks perchance be coming off?

The remote may be unmetered

And we may well be boffed!"

ACT II: SCENE X

Ucantelope then lost the fight

Fearing all his empty pews

The Archbishop prayed the rosary

While pounding back more booze

"T'is not God's will," he spat, he seethed

"Sweet Baby Zeus

I am not pleased!

Somehow I've got to have my Bardly day!

I'll show these fools how sermons work

Reel the sheep back

Jerk by jerk

'Cause Holy Smokes

I've some things to say!"

He chugged a fifth of Film Star Lite

Cried, "Cinematic dynamite!"
But started with his standard
Let us pray...

In a blaze o' beastly glory
We went down
The Barnyard call it came
And off to town
Well, there ain't no shame in saying
We's a couple o' barnyard donkeys braying
Hallelujah praise The Lord
Next time round

Hallelujah praise The Lord
Next time round
Hallelujah praise The Lord
Next time round
Next time round
In a Barnyard blaze of glory

Next time round's another story

Hallelujah praise The Lord

Next time round

In a blaze o beastly glory

We went down

There's a Barnyard hall of shame

It's all around

Oh, it's around

Well we'll catch up with religion

If we both come back as pigeons

Dropping blazing beastly glories

Next time round

No, we ain't no donkeys taking guff

These here donkeys heard just about enough

Hallelujah praise The Lord

Next time round

Next time round

In a Barnyard blaze of glory
Next time round you're gonna be sorry
Hallelujah praise The Lord
Next time round
Hallelujah praise The Lord
Next time round
Hallelujah, praise The Lord
Next tiiiime roooound!

Biscuit City folk exploded
As Ucantelope's cloth imploded
And his lunch went projectile bombs away!
He took a bow without stalling
Having found himself a brand new calling
Thespian trumps preacher any day!
After falling to his humbled floor
They hauled his daft ass out the door
Clean she howled, "Oh, that was sublime!"
"What the heck," said King Worry

"Let's hear from the final furry!"

"Oui!" said Clean

"That would be divine!"

"Anais Anon, come on, come on

"Get up there!" screamed the Duke

"You'll be bon and not alone!

Just don't slip up on the Plastered Pastor's puke!"

Anais sexy-winked at Baffled Hot

His tongue tied in a twisted knot

With temperature rising by degree

Somebody let the donkey out again!

He's naught been seen

Since just about half past ten

There's a donkey here

And a donkey there

There's a donkey runnin' round everywhere!

Somebody let the donkey out again!

Somebody let the kitty cat out again!
She's naught been seen
Since just about half past ten
There's a kitty cat here
And a kitty cat there
There's a kitty cat runnin' round everywhere!
Somebody let the kitty cat out again!

This song's for my lover boy
With a bag of Sweet Cheeks Ahoy!
Biscuits plump with chips au chocolate!
Knead and tickle, all by hand
Watch them rise up and expand
Then popped right in the oven to get fab
Fresh-baked like my half-baked baby
I shape my biscuits like his lady
I am Anais Anon, Mrs. Bafflegab!

The knight so loved his pretty pearl

He was working fast to unfurl

The tangled mess that was his swollen tongue

"Hey there, big boy!" cried Anouk

"Let Anais help you with that Marmaduke!

You're going to need it

I can tell you that for sure!

Oui, it's biscuits for her baby

And I don't mean maybe!

Biscuits for her baby everyday!"

ACT II: SCENE XI

The Duchess transformed through the night
Sensing now a changing light
Oh, the method madness of her darling Duke
Bad decisions come to all
Folly shouts
Pride doth fall
Times they change
Appearances do lie
Rantsalot had healed stage fright
But still, "Wow, this is my wedding night!"
Truth be told, he was a wee hot mess
Until a dart flew straight at the King
Rantsy dove and tipped it with his ring!
His signet R deflecting it away!

Around the arrow was a note

That was for Ucantelope!

BC now is my home, Anglais!

There was no time to boo or hiss

Antoinette and Rantsy kissed!

Well hope be gentle

Hope be kind

Rantsy was without his mind!

And angels danced

In Silver Light Unseen

The feeling that came over him

Was Holy Cow, Intrinsic Spin!

Now this was what a Knight

Could call a dream!

Antoinette my sweet, my sweet

I say we oughta write Retreat!

Together!

Shall we get ourselves a room?

"Oui oui, bebe!" she did say

"Boom-boom we go, on our way!

Down to the sea

To paddle your full moon!"

Ranting lad fell to his knees

The groundlings shouted

"Rantsy, please!

Get off the stage!

We want to hear the Earl!"

The Queen said "Not so fast out there!

I want the spake of au contraire!

Duchess get your bodice here tout suite!"

Dirty Lies went wild and shouted

"Mais Oui Clean!

No doubt about it!

Let's not debate who's Will I Am!

Give me butter bombs and sweet peach jam!

I want to mange them down right here and now!"

"What?" said Clean

"You're dreaming Witch!

Have you la-di-dah delighted?

Prithee preach, you nasty switch!

Prithee, show me how!"

ACT II: SCENE XII

The Duke and Duchess

Lost the key

To the Mannequins e-state

As the settings now'd been hacked by One

Writing Code to Heaven's Gate

But who doth hold

The Bardly Key?

Now kept beneath Upstairs

Perchance seeds sown in fallow soil?

Or a Nurse who once declared?

The poet doth awake, he does

Let your dance of love begin

Let me strip away your fears, my son

P. H. NEWCOMBE

The time is now to live

Caressing winds convey and coo
The Duke was not no new come poo
Though he had too many pockets
Filled with keys and coins and spells
But the thing with holes in pockets
Is they don't come with science rockets
And as sure as twit surpass too few brain cells
So like a dullard on a dunghill
Duke checked and checked again
And finally it doth come to him
I guess the Duchess is unchained!
Whither, hither, thither
Forswear forbear forsooth
Default defame deface
Eye for eye and tooth for tooth
Dead men's fingers poke and prod
Long purple Cupid's flower

Fairest boding like sweet sleep

Pottle pot to pottle deep

Short of shrift

On graveyard shift

Let's kick this thing in gear

From whence all this is coming

Can't say it's all to clear

Forgiveness is a funny thing

Prithee do self-righteous think?

Spare the guns, drums, fifes and wounds

Five and twenty doth go clink

So the Duchess of the soiled one

Got her turn, Lysandered Sly

And here is what came out of her

Here was her reply…

Lies Battleground shrewd berry

I flipped Henry for your Worry

Four on the forgery floor

Fur it shall not fly and soar
Quickly Mistress stuff that bun
Mark my words I'm having fun!
This Summer's Night
12 is not A Winter's Tale!

Valentine to Kinsmen
Cupid hold me to your breast
Romeo and Juliet
True labor'd love to rest
Falling staff's not for laughs
Lear's broken heart my cost
Frozen it doth thaw and melt
That sleeping minds be freed not lost

Now the Merry Wives of Am I?
Have turned another Page
Hot as a Three Buck Pistol
On July's Star-Striped Fourth Day!

Black magic?

Or… is it white?

What kind of Fool is he?

A Coward Thief

King of Cruel Grief

Orange hair flames hiss-tory!

This scribe prescribes presaging

You can't see what I do see

City's Flame coloured Solferino

Part-Time Fool will bend a knee

He doth shout it

He doth blame it

He doth lout it

He doth shame it

But in the end

Oh yes, I'll tame it!

Because Light doth set us free!

Pander not less Bawdy Bard
Lest your belly fill with burger lard
Slender ain't no Shallow Justice
Corruptio optima pessima!
The bigger be the beggar
The Fool who falls most hard!

O's sweet timeless symphony
Form be slow art fast decaying
How do I reach inside cold skin
To heal with Love where you've been staying?

I cannot enter
Push path or course
For this is not Love's Nature
Gentle persuasion, not perforce
Choose again, dear friend
A Course in Nomenclature

Veil of Maya

To Mother Gaia

How could this fancy fusion

Both separate reality

And equal part illusion

Hoodwink the Holy Ghost?

Hardly Son, I come a-laughing

Oh, bald buttered Milquetoast

My angels overstaffing

Will soon be done with all this halfing

T'il I hold you near, always close

Commune with me

Commune with us

Come and dine

Taste bread and wine

Set sail for Heaven's Coast

ACT III: SCENE I

Prince Paul and Princess Paula

Two fellow travellers here in time

Were watching from the balcony

Thinking of their own sweet rhyme

"I love you darling, yes I do"

Said Paula to her Paul

"Hey hey Paula, won't you marry me?

Babe, you know we've got it all"

"You know I will," said the pretty girl

"We can ride this whole thing out

We'll get our chance to dance and twirl

To do it all

To twist and shout!

We've got to toe the line for now"

Said she who moved so slow

"For a boy who makes excuses fast

I think you're learning how to grow"

"Should we go up there and show them how?

Make our intentions crystal clear?"

"Nah," she whispered, with a wink

"Babe, let's get out of here"

So off they went into the night

Holding hands, squeezing tight

Smiling like they'd found their special place

Attraction is a funny thing

Love is blind

Like… ding-a-ling?

Who was spinning there?

In their Inner Space

Young couple cute shared that "look"

Then skipped off to write their Absey Book

They knew Biscuit City

Needed much to change

ACT III: SCENE II

Meanwhile Small Talk Satan

Staged The Café Cheesy Whoring

He was flirting with two Fools

BS and Mighty Boring

They were driving Satan crazy

Ignoring lusty glances

They chose dumb digits and devices

Over his overt advances

He figured I must just as well

Switch to another team

That's it I'm done, said Small Talk one

Time to chase my highest dream!

I know that I was Born to Run!

To love The Big Man too!

But that'll be the day perhaps
Easier to tame a shrew!

My name is Small Talk Satan
I don't mind if I intrude
Screw peace and quiet everyone
I must provide this interlude
Of my weary mind's detritus
Speaking forth of foot and mouth
Some kind of Andronicus the Titus
Ironic monster due down South
All this sexual in-your-end, oh
So silent in the room
Fear did find its metaphor
By form of virus come too soon
There is no perfect answer
There is no perfect way
All I know is this damn cancer
Came out of nowhere one dark day

Now the elephant in the room
Is standing on a stage
I cannot speak for everyone
There's no chance
For I'm no sage
I'm no hero
I just hurt
Like all in weary world well fooled
To somehow think we're different
And we play by our own rules
Yes, I used to be a jungle cat
With muscles in my shirt
But all my buttons came undone
And I was left alone to hurt
I tripped over a cul-de-sac
Of overcompensating pain
And caught off guard
It made my style
Bubble down the drain

BS style

Goes down the drain

In a while, it's all the same

And Boring style

Is mighty lame

My uniform

It can't remain

Because in time

It's all in vain

And Small Talk style

One day goes down the drain

BS was selling lukewarm wrong

Mighty Boring smoking dumb-ass bong

Both hopped up with extra foam to go

Satan said, "Let's fill the tub!"

But nothing doing, "There's the rub!"

No way for "Lucky Bubbles, let 'er blow!"

"Are we talking gas," asked BS?

"How's the weather?" ~ Mighty Boring

"Stop!" screamed Small Talk Satan

He was on his knees imploring!

"You beat me at my own game

I'm giving up Ham's ghost!

I swear to God next time around

I'll come back as Elwy Yost!"

It was clear to him BS was lying

While the Boring one kept on trying

Now in pure hell, man, earnest praying

Hath no fun, hath no playing

For that you'd have to squeeze them hard

To get two tortured smiles out

Or drip two drams of lard

Ok, let's switch the channel

Cut To: Bored to death full gored

No mercy offered straight up now

And we mean that, My Sweet Lord

Both Fools were on their phones again

With confessions Satan feared
So he started dialing Operator
"Can you get me Jesus here?"

We have a grand confession
Of a grievance to be known
Not against you or the Big Boss
But against our own smart phone
Not that it be smart as us
'Cause that's just not the case
It' just way better organized
And can get things done at pace
Phone can be still and quiet
It's no cluttered clueless sot
It sits there still for hours
Like us waiting for a thought
It doesn't give a ring or roam
It doesn't need a hug or kiss
It doesn't need approval

Or anything like this
It just sits nice and quiet
In comfort all alone
It's got its shit together
That's why it's a real smart phone
Yes, we have a grand confession
Of a grievance to be known
Not against you or the Big Boss
But against our own smart phone
Not that it be smart as us
With that, well we could live
It's just that it now owns us
And that you can't forgive
But sorry Small Talk Satan
It's not that we don't care
It's not like you're unattractive
Or we don't see your stare
It's just that we're committed
In a relationship already

Our smart phone is our new master

And with it we're going steady

ACT III: SCENE III

You've got to eat a peck of dirt

Before you get to die

That's the way that matter is

Soiled pants and hands before we fly

The Duchess finished her best shot

Now the Duke to take a chance

Groundlings clear were swaying moved

They'd finally "got" the Bard's new dance

Worry saw his brother there

Seated on cold stage

The one he'd once been denied

Ironically the latest rage

The Duke could not feel any worse

He'd fallen to a devil's curse

And squandered precious looks, that's for sure
But in Worry's heart there was no doubt
Bad Decisions both within and out
Would regain his heart and Soul
Once held so pure

Forgiveness is the hardest thing
That anyone can learn
The one for me most hard to heal
Is myself, at every turn
You can run away like this Duke
But Life doth balk and will rebuke
The only one I ever Fooled
Was standing in my mirror
Forgiveness is the Love of God
Being neither easy nor of fear
It takes strength and courage to admit
Its Light doth shine most clear

"I think it's time to come home"

Said the Duke to brother Worry

"I've made some bad calls as you know

Haste makes waste in such a hurry

But you know, brother dear

And chosen wife of mine

T' is not too late to spin here

And turn things on a dime

And take a Chance on Fate

I hear Zoom calling from Beyond

Love is my eternal date

Love's All's homecoming song

I hear that quiet whisper coming

Yes…it's coming to me now…

It's the Prince and Princess Paula

They're re on their way right NOW!"

ACT III: SCENE IV

Paul and Paula crashed the party
Sudden "POOF" and there they be
The groundlings gasped
Twin teens unmasked
Making plain for all to see
They'd commandeered this Love-In
And they appeared a-fire set free!
The crazy kids were noble cooking
New-conceived with hearts aglow
Love being new enkindled
Biscuit City soon new-store
Everyone was shocked a-much
Mother Earth She shook with joy!
Violet Flame was burning bright above

Was it girl or was it boy?

Wrong again, dear reader

Here's another thought

Twins were in the stars for them

From another time and tale well taught

Paul and Paula took the platform

Holding in their hands

An Absey Book writ to transform

One starring two cute fans

"We aren't on social media

That's well before our time"

Said Past Prince of Sad Excuses

"But I know we sure can rhyme

We've got something here for you all

Please open up and have a look

This is about a pony and a piglet

It's our children's Absey Book!"

Once upon a time
In a world filled with rhyme
Lived a pony and a little wee pig
Well, these two were friends
And they lived on a farm
That was pretty, but not vey big
They were feisty and young
And had plenty of fun
Playing all day on the farm
One was dappled and gray
The other pink and so gay
And both were just dripping with charm
Applebert was the Pony
Wigglebob was the Pig
And you know, we're happy to say
That nowhere around
Could there ever be found
Two friends who were kinder than they
They helped out each other

Just like they were brothers
Especially when learning to read
So this is a story
Of a day in their glory
When they were learning their ABCs

It was down by the pond
On a warm afternoon
Where the two had stopped for a drink
They'd been running a lot
And were both very hot
And were feeling too tired to think
"Applebert," said his friend
"I'm pooped again… I cannot run anymore"
"Well let's take a break,
And have a drink from the lake" said the pony
Who'd heard this before
"I can't run like you
What's a poor pig to do?"

Said Wigglebob to his good pal

"My legs are too short

And I huff and I snort

And I feel like I'm having a cow!"

Applebert understood

Because when it came to food

He couldn't eat like his plump little chummy

Though try as he may

There had yet been a day

He'd put half as much food in his tummy

"Don't worry," he said

"There's nothing to dread

You're doing the best that you can

We can't all run swift

So please don't be miffed

I'm still you're number one fan!"

Wigglebob nodded his head

Thought, and then said,

"You know, I think you are right

I can't run too well
But at eating I'm swell
And right now I could sure use a bite!"
Applebert shook his head
"I'm so sorry," he said
"There's nothing around here to eat
And we've a long way to roam
Before we get home
To get you a lovely treat"
"Please Applebert, it's starting to hurt!
I'm hungry, I'm starving!" he cried
"But I'm too tired to run
Oh, what can be done?
Oh dear oh me dear oh me my"
"Relax Wigglebob, I'm spot on the job
I'll think of something with ease
I've got it" he shouted!
While Wigglebob pouted
"Let's practice our ABCs!"

"Let me go first
After quenching our thirst"
Said the pony about to get wet
"We'll each name a food
That we think is good
Taking turns through the alphabet"
Well the mere mention of food
Changed Wigglebob's mood
And he got all excited again
"Okay, Applebert, I guess it can't hurt
You know, I love you my friend!"
The pair laughed aloud
And they both felt so proud
To be together on such a fine day
So they took a long drink
Then started to think
And here's what they had to say:

"A" is for Apples, cried Applebert

My teeth will love me for this!

And "B" is for beans! said Wigglebob

Pinch you nose and give me a kiss!

"C" is for carrots! I love them I do!

I could eat them every day!

And "D" is for dumplings!

Swimming in soup!

Give me more! Give me more I do say!

"E" is for eggs, sunny-side up

We can thank our neighbors, the hens

And "F" is for flapjacks

I can't get enough!

Especially with syrup on them!

"G" is for gravy!

Thick as mud

Now you know a lot about that

Yes and "H" is for honey

Which I'd take over money

And nary an eyelash I'd bat!

"I" is for lovely icicles!

Frozen water that I love to lick

And "J" is for jello!

My favorite is yellow!

I just wish it came by the brick!

"K" is for kernels

Of corn, I might add

My friend Wigglebob loves them for sure!

Oh yes, Applebert!

Did Wigglebob blurt

They are golden and sweet and so pure!

"L" is for lettuce!

Green as the grass

That Applebert grazes with grace!

And "M"'s for the treat we know as molasses

Oh how it sticks to your face!

"N" is for nuts

Of varying kinds

So tiny and tasty and good

An "O" is for oats!

That I love to eat

And it's not just because I should!

"P" is for pepper

How it makes us sneeze

If we snort just a little too much

And "Q" is for quiche!

More eggs if you please

With mushrooms and cheese and such!

"R" is for raisins!

Well deserving our praisin'!

'Cause they're dried and sweet as can be!

And "S" is for sugar!

Which I love by the lump

But I take mine without any tea!

Well Wigglebob squealed aloud with delight

And he wiggled his round little fanny

And Applebert whinnied

And threw back his mane

With style that was truly uncanny!

"T" is for turnips!

Said the cute little piggy

But never to eat as dessert

Like "U"

As in upside down

It's good cake!

Made with pineapple, Applebert!

No fair said the pony

I missed a turn

But that's okay 'cause your rhyming was great

Like "V" as in vegetables

Of which there are many

Too many to name as it's late

And "W"s for watermelon

Which kind of brings us back to our drink

And "X" is for extra helpings I guess

'Cause there's no foods of which I can think!

You're right, Applebert, we're nearing the end
And yogurt begins with a "Y"
And "Z"'s for zucchini!
And yes, my good friend
We finished it, you and I!

Well they'd had so much fun
They were ready to run
Cause Wigglebob felt a lot better
They'd finished their ABCs for the day
And covered all twenty-six letters!
Wigglebob now was filled with resolve
And he took off like a going concern
His little legs churned as fast they could
And his muscles they ached and they burned
While Applebert ambled along by his side
Trotting as slow as can be
Encouraging Wigglebob as he went
While shading him like a tree

So they ran and they ran and they ran some more
And soon the farm was in sight
"You can do it my friend
We're nearing the end
Give it all your piggily might!"
And when they made it back home
To the farm at last
Wigglebob squealed with glee
"I made it," he cried!
"With my friend by my side
Oh wiggily piggily wheee!
Thanks Applebert!
You know I'd give you the shirt
Off my back if actually wore one
And I'd give you a hug
You big handsome lug
But you are nearly as tall as the Sun!"
"No problem, little Buddy!
You'd get me all muddy!

With those hooves all covered in guck!
And give yourself credit
You did it yourelf
I was just there in case you got stuck!"
Now Wigglebob's heart was filled with pride
And love for his wonderful friend
So he asked Applebert to come closer
And waited for the pony to bend
When Applebert's head
Was down near the ground
Wigglebob whispered, "Listen to this"
But when he turned his head
Applebert heard nothing said
Except the smack of a big juicy kiss!
Applebert blushed
"Well thank you so much!
I really don't know what to say
It was fun helping you
And you helped me too

You know, we had a really great day!"
The piglet agreed
It was a fine day indeed
So they promised to it again
"Tomorrow," they said
"After supper and bed
And let's hope that it just doesn't rain!"

ACT III: SCENE V

King Worry and Queen Super Clean
Let out a shrill-gorged cry!
They shrieked YES in perfect harmony!
No prophetic fury
No asking why
They knew their son and daughter
Were in truth the perfect match
There could be no other answer
To a locked and loaded latch
They could sense March-chicks a bit affright
So they smiled with eyes that knew
"Mom and Dad," said Princess Paula
"Yes, we've got some news, it's true
We're expecting, and we're much in love

Just like the two of you!"

Prince Paul next, he did say

"The time was not our choice

But accidents do happen

And we're so thankful you rejoice!

And will give what's needed henceforth, but

What of others who be poorer?

Those with naught same help or voice?"

Said Paula, loud and clear

"There are those in Biscuit City

Who are hungry and sleep with much to fear!

Some are starved, some out of wedlock

Some without home trying to survive!

We see them every day here

Their life's an unfair fight to be alive!"

"There is no place here," Paul said

"No kingdom where all needs get met

And we hope that you and mother

Will be kind and not forget

We want to be extra great

Like Sir Lingo and the Earl

We know we went behind your backs

But do forgive your lovely pearls

We told them what we want to do

And we have their wisdom much to thank

Mom…

Dad…

It would make us glad

Can we create a new food bank?"

"Yes, The Biscuit City Food Bank!"

Said Paula, "Is our wedding wish!

We could fill the plates of everyone

Every Biscuit City dish!

That could be our brand new job!

We could work like everyone!

Not just hang out looking pretty

You know, we feel like royal bums!

So what perchance Mom and Pop

Do you think about all this?

We know it must be quite a shock

But can we seal it with a kiss?

If we win the prize of butter bombs

The croissants will be shared

With everyone who's here now

And more can be prepared

We have the world's best bun maker!

Her name Is Jolie St. Germaine!

God she bakes like she's insane

And she's our Biscuit City Baker!"

ACT III: SCENE VI

Jolie now had left her kitchen
Made her way up onto stage
With apron style rad bitchin'
Red hair styled wow awesome rage
French was she rouge, blanc et bleu
Statuesque, strong and tall
And the C on her apron said
Les Canadiens de Montreal!
"Are you Puck or Bottom?"
She sang-shouted to the crowd!
She cupped her hand to her ear
"C'mon let's hear you loud!"
The groundlings roared approval
Half were Bottom, half were Puck!

On a Dreamy Night Midsummer
Who could ask for better luck?
"Now don't go getting prissy!
Or sissy or be square!
Are you enjoying all my croissants?
Are you having fun out there?!
Je suis Jolie St. Germaine!
And where be smoke, oui, be fire!
Now here's a special treat for you
Advice and Lingo Clarifier!"

The Earl of Good Advice
Was a man the King did trust
He loved him like Will Ferrell
Dropping good old Mark Twain's bust!
Young early Earl had many sides
Yes, most were fueled by lust
Sometimes he made mistakes, like all
And sometimes he simply fussed

His head had handled many Pucks
Made his brain go woe to golly shucks!
Still underneath all of this
Something there was pure
Despite confidence a-lacking
Spiff and polish poor man sure
Patience is the kingly way
Never give up on your son
And then it happened one good day
He ascended to the One
The Light came on Page 7
Out in a Veiled Greenfield
He sauntered off to Heaven
Baptized by the Dove's Light Shield
When he came back home to Gaia
Things had changed but still a jerk
So he rolled up two green sleeves
Went out in Whitman's yard to work
Now the monarchs sat a-waiting

To see what would transpire

When in a flash before them came

Advice and Lingo Clarifier!

Holding hands and laughing

Was plain to see they were a pair!

Love and Glee

Were there to see

Yes, was plain to see

Love and Glee

Were making history!

They took to stage and shouted

"Man, let's get this good job done!

There's no use in denying it

Two hearts trump only one!"

So back and forth their voices

From two hearts burst forth and rang

They knew all about wise choices

And this is what they sang…

God seems to work through people
More often than not
Sometimes He works through angels
Sometimes She herself gets caught
In the Act of Creation
With a brushstroke of color
More wondrous than any artist ever wrought

Have you ever watched the Moon?
In a clear and starlit summer sky
As she bathes herself in silver light
So beautiful it makes the angels cry
And just around the corner
On this spinning Mother Earth
The Sun is also rising
As She reflects His Light of Truth

And the teardrops of the angels
Are dried and turned to smiles

In Miracles of Kindness

Bringing food to the poorest little child
The teardrops of the angels
Are dried and turned to smiles
In miracles of kindness
Bringing help to the sickest little child

God seems to work through people
More often than not
And miracles of kindness
Are here for us to give
Like the angels that whisper to us
Through feeling and in thought

God seems to work through people
More often than not
And miracles of kindness
Are in our hands right now
So let's share all the love and kindness

All the miracles that Heaven Will Allow
And the teardrops of the angels
Are dried and turned to smiles
In miracles of kindness
Bringing hope to the bravest little child

And the teardrops of the angels
Are dried and turned to smiles
In miracles of kindness
Bringing Love to the poorest little child

ACT III: SCENE VII

Small Talk Satan now was full

Of BS and Mighty Boring

So he hatched a plan to sail away

While BC Love was full out-pouring

He slipped off sneaky weasel-like

Scurried down to Biscuit Bay

Where he stole the Maid of Driftwood

And set sail for Dauphine?

He figured ask her for a date

Perhaps she is my dinghy mate?

But the thing that zipped past Beelzebub

Was driftwood's just debris

Great with ducky in the tub

But unfit to sail high seas

Now frothing at the mouth he sailed
Lucky Bubbles not so much
Small Talk Satan sunk the Driftwood
His uncertain Fate sealed nonesuch
Back in Biscuit City
The King and Queen and everyone
Were dancing underneath the stars
Having named no Champion!
No one seemed to care a bit
As Love won all in the end
But don't kid yourself about it
And damn straight don't pretend
Here but for God's Grace we go
And we will all go in truth
If your wish is to be free and know
Forsake forswear forsooth
There's so much good here left to do
While learning memory doth lie
This dream you're dreaming surely ends

So have fun, do laugh, do cry

Live life to its fullest

Find what's right for you

Invent when and what that should be

And how best that you should try

Just know all your choices govern

With whom and where you next doth flye!

ACT III: SCENE VIII

He was a long time watching

The way that She looked

And the way

That She set her stare

He sometimes wondered am I just imagining

Or am I right?

And she truly does care

You know they say that the eyes

Are the windows of the Soul

And yes, I believe that it's true

If you've been looking in mine

Then I'm sure that you know

I'm head over heels

In love with you

You never knew who I was

But now I AM, I AM

We are given endless choice and chance

Until spinning Light in Heaven's Dance

Will wrote All's Well that Ends Well

But nothing really ends

One door begets another

Birth to death

Let's make amends

One day it just comes to you

In a moment of pure Grace

Your heart and breath up-taken

As you gaze at Glory's Face

The Light is blinding

Warmth unreal

And Awe's the only word

That could come close to naming Heaven

When we leave this broken world

I love you all

I love you so

Wish I did not have to go

But my time is near

I feel it close

I call to you

I know

I know

I hear you darling

Feel you near

Eyes filled with tears

We merge in Joy

Caress me with your fingertips

Spiral higher country boy!

I never want to stop this dance

Kiss me with your Violet Breath

Where nothing's lost

Or left to chance

Where we find Union long past death

Where You are Moon

And I am Sun

Forever Twinned

Our Soul is One

Where I am Moon

And you are Sun

Forever Twinned

Our Soul is One

I give now

This pledge to Thee

My Heart is Yours

Eternally

Epilogue

I throw thee down a gauntlet

Now let's really "Cut to Chase"

The mystery of … **WHO IS THE BARD?**

In Biscuit City's new web space!

To find out what the answer is

Here is where to go!

www.thebardofbisuitcity.com

Please cast a vote

Please only one

Let's see who is with my mission!

On New Year's Eve this year

As 2019 ends …

Do you have 20/20 VISION?

Please tell me who the Bard is

In this my mystery tale

And please donate to a local food bank

And help change this world full-scale ☺

(Thank you for reading. I hope you laughed. I hope you cried. I hope I made you feel alive! ~ The Bard of BC.)

Dedication

In Memory of Sharon Lee Watts

(BLUEZOOM)

February 1957 - November 1984

TO THE BRIGHTEST STAR IN THE SKY

Bluezoom

No I don't drink the whiskey

And I don't smoke the weed

I've got something stronger

Doctor says it's all I need

To keep me up and happy

Get me through the day

He says take two blue pills and lie down

And the pain just goes away…

Bluezoom

Bluezoom

I'm so far away from you

In the wind your voice it whispers help me

But there's nothing I can do

Sleep is miles away from me

And I'm so far away from you

Sleep is miles away from me

And I'm so far away from you

Bluezoom

It was 30 years ago back in 1984
On a cold November night
My heart was broke forevermore
I said goodbye in silence
Standing crying in the rain
I've been wandering lost and lonely since
No, nothing's ever been the same
Bluezoom

I see a blue ring up there in the sky
Slipped around the silver moon
You were only 27
You left us all too soon
I see you in the stars at night
I hold you in my dreams
You're always right here in my heart
Your love is calling like a blue moonbeam

No I don't drink the whiskey

And I don't smoke the weed

I've got something stronger

Doctor says it's all I need

To keep me actin' happy

Chase these crazy blues away

I take two blue pills he gives me

But the pain don't go away

Bluezoom

No, it never goes away

Bluezoom

Bluezoom

I'm so far away from you

In the wind your voice it whispers help me

But there's nothing I can do

Sleep is miles away from me

And I'm so far away from you

Sleep is miles away from me

And I'm so far away from you

Bluezoom

Bluezoom

Blue Bluezoom

Paul ~ November 15, 2014

Acknowledgements

First, I thank my parents, Raymond and Kathleen. I owe my wonderful life to them. Love you forever, as well as my brother, Brad, daughter, Olivia, and extended family.

Thank you to Julie and Greg Salisbury of Influence Publishing for acknowledging my work and guiding me through the publishing process.

Brien Miron, Jim Shield, Ralph Walker, Sam Robert Muik, Steven Cree Molison and Professor Shona Ellis, thank you for your testimonials. I'm honored.

Rick Cepella, a fine Canadian painter whose work reminds me much of John Singer Sargent, thank you for your words of support.

Others I would like to thank are: the late Larry Plager, Laurie Plager, Margaret Rapkoski, Stephen McCorry, Barbara Banfield, Patrick & Alyssa Moran, Margaret Bellaty, Monica Normandeau, Luca Maraschi & Julia Cherkassky, Claire Monash, Craig Addy, Michelle Cho, Ruta Semeniukaite,

Carol Cockrum, Anthony Norfolk, Sara Alexander, Claude Tremblay, Ben Burcat Dogan, Tim & Hilary Temple, Karly DeGroot, Pat Donovan, Amy Blake, Mahrouyeh Maghzi, Andrea Iapaolo, Tonia Wa, Shehnaz Hozaima, Bill & Joanne Medeot, Chris Medeot, Ladan Mojallal, Chris, Christina & Forest Glover, Janet Leduc, Gerry Casavant, Laurrie Zechoval, Jina Lim and her wonderful staff at JJ Bean, and a young feathered friend called Jordan the Seagull. You all inspire me.

Last, but not least, thanks to Delrae Fawcett for bringing sweet jam to the "office" and brightening many writing days with laughter and gentle wisdom.

And special thanks to Mr. Elvis Costello for his song, *Everyday I Write the Book*. I have no idea how many times I listened to it while cooking up these words in the loft.

To anyone I forgot to mention, apologies, you know who you are and how you helped me.

I'm grateful. And see you soon, my dear guiding Angel of Light.

P. H. Newcombe

Vancouver, B.C

March 24, 2019

About the Author

P. H. Newcombe was born and raised near Ottawa. He played hockey and studied journalism, psychology and counselling in college. He worked for many years in services for people with a variety of disabilities and challenges and people who are chronically mentally ill and homeless. He also worked with the City of Toronto in the Community Services Department and with the Information and Communications Division of the Chief Administrative Officer's Department. Paul lives in Vancouver and is a writer, actor, and photographer. He has authored four as yet unproduced screenplays, *Hanna's Story*, *Slowpoke*, *The Universal Mind* and a mini-series adaptation of Ernest Buckler's *The Mountain and the Valley*. *The Bard of Biscuit City: A Romantic New Age Mystery Rhyme* is his first book of fiction and poetry. He will be promoting the book leading up to New Year's Eve 2019, when the identity of the Bard of Biscuit City will be revealed online to set his stage for a new "2020" vision. Please visit his website for additional information.

www.thebardofbiscuitcity.com

author@thebardofbiscuitcity.com

Facebook: The Bard of Biscuit City